beehive

Jorey Hurley

A Paula Wiseman Book
Simon & Schuster Books for Young Readers
New York London Toronto Sydney New Delhi

buzz

swarm

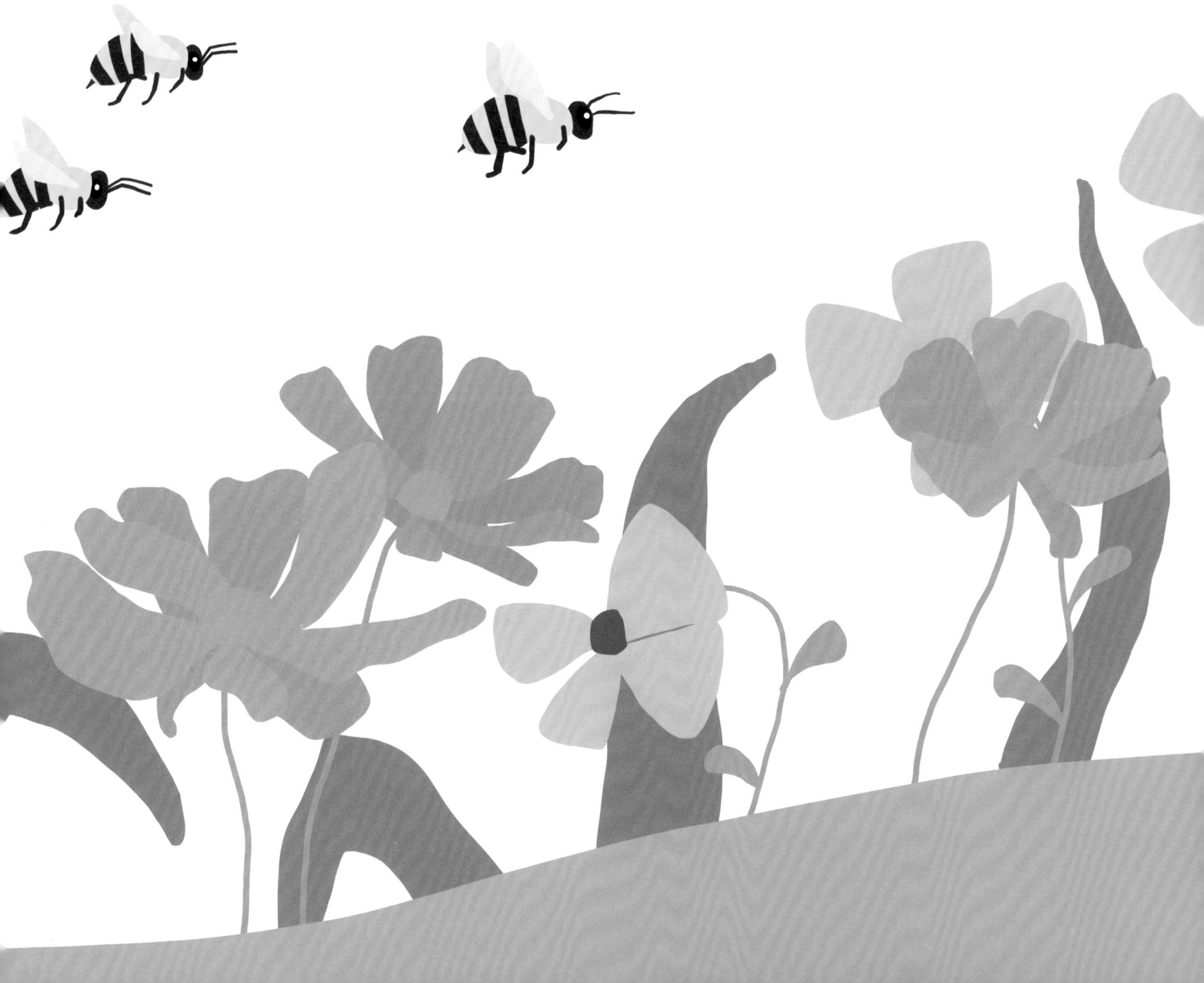

explore

find

build

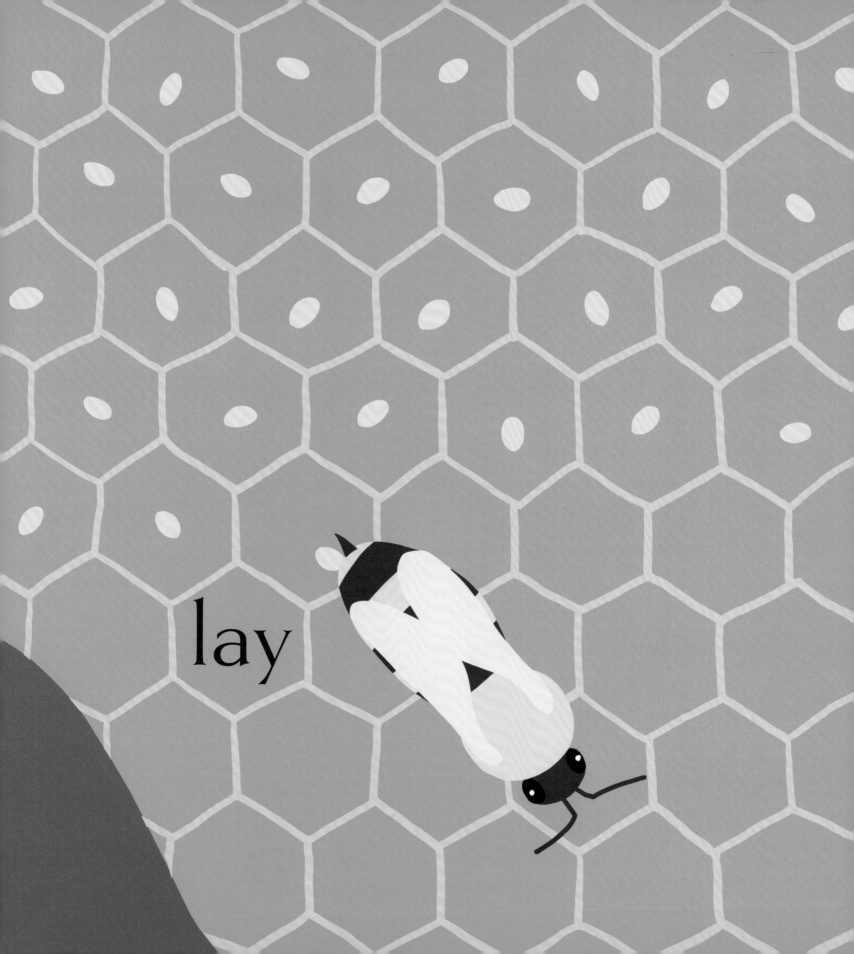

lay

feed

grown

fly

collect

pollinate

guard

sting

keep

honey

for Alder and Holden

SIMON & SCHUSTER BOOKS FOR YOUNG READERS • An imprint of Simon & Schuster Children's Publishing Division • 1230 Avenue of the Americas, New York, New York 10020 • Copyright © 2020 by Jorey Hurley • All rights reserved, including the right of reproduction in whole or in part in any form. • SIMON & SCHUSTER BOOKS FOR YOUNG READERS is a trademark of Simon & Schuster, Inc. • For information about special discounts for bulk purchases, please contact Simon & Schuster Special Sales at 1-866-506-1949 or business@simonandschuster.com. • The Simon & Schuster Speakers Bureau can bring authors to your live event. For more information or to book an event, contact the Simon & Schuster Speakers Bureau at 1-866-248-3049 or visit our website at www.simonspeakers.com. • Book design by Lizzy Bromley • The text for this book was set in Goldenbook. • The illustrations for this book were rendered in Photoshop. • Manufactured in China • 1019 SCP • First Edition • 10 9 8 7 6 5 4 3 2 1 • Library of Congress Cataloging-in-Publication Data • Names: Hurley, Jorey, author. • Title: Beehive / Jorey Hurley. • Description: First edition. | New York : Simon & Schuster Books for Young Readers, [2020] | "A Paula Wiseman Book." | Audience: Ages 3-7. | Audience: K to grade 3. • Identifiers: LCCN 2019006386 | ISBN 9781481470032 (hardcover) | ISBN 9781481470049 (e-book) • Subjects: LCSH: Beehives—Juvenile literature. | Honeybee—Juvenile literature. | Bee culture—Juvenile literature. • Classification: LCC SF532 .H867 2020 | DDC 595.79/9—dc23 LC record available at https://lccn.loc.gov/2019006386

author's note

The sound we hear as BUZZ is caused by a bee's rapid wingbeats vibrating the surrounding air. A queen bee and a large group of worker bees that leave an old hive in search of a site for a new one are called a SWARM. After leaving the old hive, the group will wait in one place while scout bees EXPLORE the nearby area to find a new hive site. When the scouts FIND a hollow tree or other good spot for their new hive, they tell the group about it through a special dance that explains the location of the site. The bees BUILD a nest by making honeycombs out of wax they make in their own abdomens. They attach the honeycombs to the top and sides of the hollow area.

In the hive, the queen bee will LAY one tiny egg in each cell of the honeycomb. After three days, each egg hatches into a larva, which looks like a short, white worm. The worker bees FEED the larvae, which have big appetites and eat more than a thousand times a day. After five days, the worker bees cover the top of each larva's cell with a wax cap. Now the larvae become pupae. Over the next thirteen days, the pupae's bodies change, until they are ready to emerge as full-GROWN honeybees.

Honeybees FLY by flapping their wings 230 times per second in short, rotating strokes. They travel far from the hive to COLLECT liquid nectar and particles of pollen from a wide variety of flowering plants. As they move from plant to plant, they POLLINATE the flowers by leaving behind little bits of pollen from flowers visited earlier.

Some bees stay near the hive to GUARD it from predators such as bears and skunks. When they discover a threat, they emit a smell that warns the other bees and then STING the intruder. The sharp, hooked stinger will stick in a mammal's skin and rip off part of the bee's body, which causes the honeybee to die after stinging.

Honeybees inside the hive KEEP the nectar collected from outside and turn it into HONEY. The bees in the hive eat some honey themselves and feed some to the growing larvae, but it is particularly important to have a big reserve for winter when there aren't any flowering plants around. A hive with tens of thousands of bees can use up to thirty pounds of stored honey over a cold winter as they wait for spring flowers to return.

Bee populations, both wild and domestic, have been declining in recent decades. Scientists believe this is because of habitat loss, pesticide use, invasive species, climate change, and diseases such as colony collapse disorder, in which all the worker bees suddenly abandon the queen and leave the hive. Many people across the world are working hard to help bees by conserving land and improving habitats for them.